Enid Blyton's

Treasure Trove

This is a Parragon Book

Parragon
13-17 Avonbridge Trading Estate
Atlantic Road, Avonmouth, Bristol. BS11 9QD
Produced by The Templar Company plc,
Pippbrook Mill, London Road, Dorking,Surrey. RH4 1JE

These stories were first published in Sunny Stories,
Teacher's Treasury, Two Years in the Infant School, Read to Us,
New Friends and Old or The Daily Mail Annual.

Printed in Italy

ISBN 0-75252-365-1

Enid Blyton's
Treasure Trove

PARRAGON

This book
belongs to

_____

_____

Contents

Enid Blyton's
The Fairy Kitten

ILLUSTRATED BY KATE DAVIES

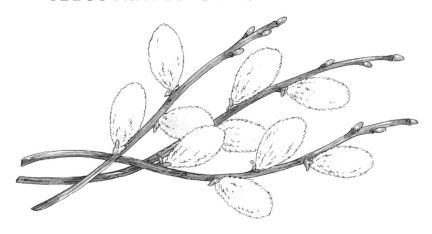

There was once a little boy called John. He lived with his mother and father in a lovely little cottage at the edge of the woods. Usually he was a happy little boy, who laughed and played all day in the sunshine, but just lately he had been very unhappy because his little grey kitten had run away and got lost.

John had looked everywhere for her – in the house, in the garden, in the summer house, in the garage and in the road.

"She may have run into the wood," said his mother. "Go and see if you can find her there, John."

So off John went to the woods where primroses and celandines were flowering, and where the silver pussy willow shone pale and soft in the warm spring sun.

But his kitten was nowhere to be found, and John could have cried with disappointment. He had so loved playing with her. He was sure he would never find another kitten that was as pretty as she was.

Suddenly he stopped still and listened. Was that a mew that he heard?

Surely it was!

The noise came again softly, very high and quiet, not exactly like a mew, but John couldn't think what else it could be. He began looking about to see where the noise came from. It sounded as though it came from somewhere low down.

Yes, it came from the middle of a prickly gorse bush! Surely his poor little kitty couldn't be in there!

"Kitty! Kitty!" he called, peeping into the bush.

A little high voice answered him.

"Oh, help me, please. I'm caught in the prickles!"

John was so surprised to hear the tiny voice, that he could hardly speak.

"Who are you?" he asked at last.

"I'm a pixie-piper," said the little voice. "The wind blew me right off my feet and landed me here, and I can't get out! Will you help me?"

"A pixie!" said John excitedly.

"Yes, I'll help you! I've never seen a pixie before! But, oh my! It's rather prickly!"

He put his hands right into the gorse bush and pressed back the branches. There, in the middle, was a tiny pixie, dressed in red and yellow. Carefully John lifted him out of the bush and set him down on the ground.

"Oh, thank you!" cried the pixie. "You are kind to help me, but look at your poor hands. They are covered in scratches and scrapes. And why do you look so unhappy?"

"I'm upset because I've lost my kitten," said John sadly, and told the little pixie all about it.

"Dear, dear, that's very sad!" said the piper. "But don't worry, I'll help you. I think I know where your kitten may be. The fairies love kittens. If they've found yours, they'll have changed her into a fairy kitten. She won't be very far away. But we will have to use some pixie magic to find her. Have you ever seen a fairy kitten?"

"No, but I'd *love* to," said John excitedly. "Where are they kept?"

"There's plenty over there!" laughed the pixie-piper, pointing to a big pussy willow.

John looked. He could only see a

bush with soft, silvery buds growing all over it.

The pixie took up his pipe, and softly he began to play a lovely tune, looking at the pussy willow bush all the time.

John looked too, and he saw a
wonderful sight – so wonderful he
could hardly believe his eyes! For
the silver pussy willow buds had

changed into tiny, furry kittens, and
one by one they all scrambled
down the branches to the ground
and ran up to the piper.

They danced and frisked round
him, and ran after their little tails,
for all the world like real kittens.
The piper stopped playing
on his pipe.

"Now," he said, "you have to find your kitten. Which one is she? Quick! Can you see her? You must find her before they all go back to the tree and turn into pussy willow again!"

John ran after them,
and picked up a little
silvery kitten small enough
to fit into a nutshell!
He had found his kitty!

Then he watched the others climb up the branches and one by one turn into soft, silvery buds again!

The piper blew his pipe once more, and John's kitten grew bigger and bigger until it was just the right size.

"There you are!" said the pixie. "Don't tell anyone it's a fairy kitten. They won't believe you. Thank you for helping me, and I'm glad I've been able to help you in return. Goodbye."

He vanished, and left John alone with his fairy kitten. He ran home as fast as he could.

"Why, John!" cried his mother, "so you've found your kitty after all! I *am* glad!"

John told heaps of people how he found his fairy kitten – but the pixie was right, nobody believed him. Not even his best friend, Robert.

He didn't mind. He knew what nobody else did – and that was the place where fairy kittens come from!

And next time you see pussy willow, have a good look at it. I think you will say it's no wonder the fairies made kittens from such soft furry buds!

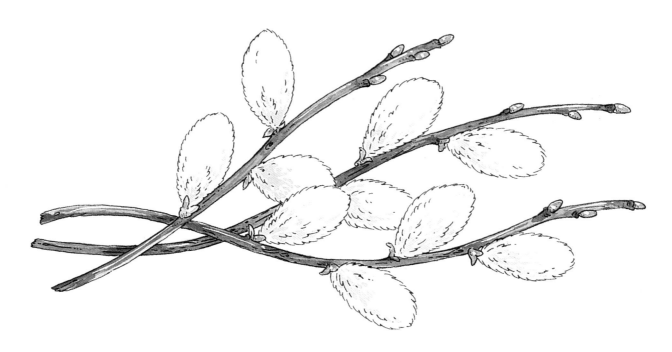

Enid Blyton's
The Silver Merman

ILLUSTRATED BY KIM RAYMOND

John was down by the seashore with his cousin Ella. He had been busy building sandcastles, when suddenly he noticed that Ella was crying.

"What's the matter, Ella?" he asked, throwing down his spade, and running over to her.

"I have lost my lovely ring," she sobbed.

"Where did you lose it?" asked John. "Let's go and hunt for it. I'm sure it won't take long to find."

"It's no use," said Ella, drying her eyes. "I lost it when I was out in the boat this morning. It fell off my finger as I was trailing my hand in the water, and before I could do anything, I saw it sinking down to the bottom of the sea."

"If only I knew the way there, I'd go and hunt for your ring," said John. "But I would drown if I went deep into the water."

"Of course you would, silly," said Ella, smiling. "Carry on building castles, and forget about my ring!"

John went off and thought hard as he dug in the sand.

"I'm sure I'd find that ring, if I could find someone to guide me under the sea," he said to himself.

"Well, I'll take you if you like!" said a sweet voice near him. John looked up in surprise. He saw a fairy sitting on a rock, with long hair blowing in the wind.

"I've never seen a fairy before!" he cried in delight. "Are you really a fairy?"

"Yes, really," she answered. "I'm on my way to visit my sister Pinkity, who married a merman. I heard what you said, as I was flying by, and I wondered if you'd like to come with me."

"Oh I *would*!" cried John. "Do please take me."

"Come along then," said the fairy,

holding out her hand. "My name's Sylfai. What's yours?"

"John," said the little boy. "That's my cousin Ella over there. She lost her ring in the waves, and I want to go down to the bottom of the sea, so that I can look for it."

Sylfai led him into the water,

and it splashed over his socks. "Oh, dear, I'll get wet!" he said. "I won't drown, will I?"

"Oh, I forgot," said Sylfai. "I must rub you with a sea-spell, so that you can walk beneath the water safe and dry. What a good thing you reminded me!"

She put her hands in the water, and then made an outline around John's body, singing strange magic words as she did so.

"There! Now you'll be all right!" she said. "Come along."

They ran into the water, deeper and deeper, until John was right up to his waist. It wasn't at all difficult to walk in the sea, like it usually is. Soon he was up to his shoulders, and then suddenly his head went right under! But he didn't splutter or choke. It was just as easy breathing in the water as on the land. John thought it was really

wonderful. Bright fish swam all around them, and beautiful seaweed floated everywhere.

"We've a long way to go, so we'll find a fish to ride on," said Sylfai.

She beckoned to a
big codfish, and soon she and
John were sitting comfortably on its
back, racing through the water.
Swish! Swish!

"I'm a little tired now," said the codfish at last. "Look, there's a crowd of jellyfish! Catch hold of the ribbons that hang down from them, and they'll carry you as far as you want to go!"

"Take us to Pinkity, the Silver Merman's wife!" cried Sylfai. The jellyfish moved off quickly, and soon they arrived at a lovely cave, where a fairy sat combing out her long hair.

Sylfai let go of the jellyfish, and ran to kiss her little sister. John followed her, feeling rather shy.

"Oh, Sylfai, how lovely to see you!" cried Pinkity. "And who is this with you?"

"This is John," said Sylfai. "He's come to look for a lovely ring that his cousin has lost in the sea."

"But the sea is such a big place – it would take him all his life to find it!" cried Pinkity. "Never mind, John, maybe you could take her a pretty piece of coral instead."

"Where's your husband?" asked Sylfai.

"Oh, he's gone to the Ocean Market," said Pinkity. "He'll be back soon, in time for tea."

She set a cloth on a rock, and put a jug of pretty seaweed in the middle. Then she put shells for plates, and cups made of pink coral. John couldn't think how anyone could drink out of a cup when there was water all around, but Sylfai said it was quite easy when you knew how! John was looking forward to trying.

Soon the meal was ready, and they took their places at the table. There was seaweed soup, pink and green jelly made from sea anemones, and starfish cakes. John was very hungry and, though he had never had such a strange meal before, he enjoyed it very much.

"Here's my husband!" cried Pinkity. John looked up, and saw a fine big merman swimming through the water. He had a tail like a fish, and gleamed like silver as he swam into the cave.

"Why, here's quite a party!" he chuckled. "Who's our guest?"

"I'm John," said John. "I'm
very pleased to meet you."
"Same to you," said the
merman, and he sat
down at the table,
and helped himself
to some jelly. He
was very friendly,
and he told John
such funny stories
about the fish

and crabs, that the little boy could hardly eat for laughing. "I bought you a present at the market, Pinkity," said the merman. It's something very special indeed! I paid a great many shells for it." "Oh, show me!" cried Pinkity. The merman opened his hand and showed them a beautiful ring.

John cried out in astonishment! "Why, it's the very ring that my cousin Ella lost! It really is!"

"Dear me, is that so?" asked the merman. "It came down from the surface of the water this morning, and was taken to the market to be sold by the fish who found it."

"Yes, and Ella lost hers this morning!" cried John. "So it must be the same one. What a very peculiar thing!"

"Well, you must take it back to Ella," said Pinkity. "I couldn't keep it now I know that."

"Oh, no," said John, "your husband bought it, and he must give it to you. I'll tell Ella, and I'm sure she'll be pleased when she knows you have got it."

"No, you must take it," said the merman.

But John wouldn't, no matter how they begged him to. He was

quite sure Ella would rather
Pinkity had it.

"I really ought to go back now,"
he said. "Ella will be worried."

"I'll take you to the shore on
one of my white horses!" said
the merman. "They go very
fast indeed."

He swam off, and soon came
back with a beautiful horse, whose
white mane streamed like foam in
the water.

"I never knew that the white waves
I saw rolling in to shore were really
and truly the manes of horses!"
said John in surprise.

The merman helped him up, and then sat on the horse behind him sideways, for his tail was rather awkward to manage on horseback.

"Goodbye!" called John, waving to Sylfai and Pinkity.

The white horse rose to the surface of the water and then, with its foamy mane just showing above the waves, began to gallop along swiftly.

Poor Ella had suddenly missed

John, and was dreadfully worried about him. She was walking up and down by the sea, calling him. A host of little fish put their heads above the water and told her not to worry, but of course she couldn't understand a word they said. She wasn't under a sea-spell, like John.

The white horse rushed out on the beach, and John jumped off. Before he could call goodbye and thank the merman, the horse

had turned, and vanished once more. John went to look for Ella.

There she was, way along the beach, calling at the top of her voice: "John, John, where are you?"

"Here I am!" called John, and he raced up to her.

"Oh, John, where have you been?" asked Ella. "I have been so worried about you."

"I've been to the bottom of the sea to look for your ring," said John.

"And do you know, the Silver Merman had bought it for Pinkity! They wanted me to take it to you, but I said I knew you would much rather Pinkity had it, and I made them keep it."

"What are you talking about?" said Ella.

"Don't tell stories, John! Nobody can go to the bottom of the sea, except divers."

"But I did go!" said John sticking his hands into his pockets, as he always did when he was cross.

"Well, I don't believe you," said Ella. "You've just been hiding somewhere to give me a fright."

"I haven't," said John – and then a strange look came over his face. He had felt something peculiar at the bottom of one of his pockets. He pulled it out – and dear me – there was the ring!

"Goodness!" he said, in astonishment. "The merman must have slipped it into my pocket when I was in front of him on the white horse!

Look Ella!
Here's your ring – now
I expect you'll believe
me, won't you!"
Ella took the ring
with a cry of
delight, and slipped
it on her finger.
"I shall have to
believe you!" she said.
"You really are a dear
to find it for me!"

Then off they went together, and John spent the rest of the day telling Ella all about his exciting adventures with his new friends under the sea.

Enid Blyton's

Look Out Busy-Body!

ILLUSTRATED BY ANGELA KINCAID

Busy-Body the elf was always poking his nose into everything. He knew everyone's business, and told everyone's secrets. He was a perfect little nuisance.

He peeped here and poked there. If Dame Twig had a new hen, he knew all about it. If Mr Round had a new hat he knew exactly what it was like, and where it was from. He was a real little busybody, so his name was a very good one.

One day Madam Soapsuds came to live in Chestnut Village, where Busy-Body's cottage was. She arrived in a small van, labelled 'Laundry Goods. With Very Great Care.' She wouldn't let the removal men unpack the van, telling them she wished to do it herself.

Busy-Body was very curious, of course. Why should she want to unpack the van herself? Was there something magic in it that she didn't want anyone else to see? He decided to hide in the front garden, and watch till Madam Soapsuds took out whatever was in that little van.

That night, before the moon was up, Madam Soapsuds came out into the garden, and went over to the van. But before she opened the door, she

said a little magic rhyme:
    "If anyone is hiding,
    They must go a-riding,
    On this witch's stick."
    She tossed an old broomstick onto
the floor. Though he tried to escape
it, it swept poor Busy-Body out from
behind the bush where he was hiding,
and carried him up into the air,
feeling very frightened indeed.
    "Ho, ho!" said Madam Soapsuds.
"I had an idea you were trying to

poke your silly little nose into my business, Busy-Body. Better stay away from me. I keep my secrets!"

So, while Busy-Body rose high above the village, Madam Soapsuds quickly and quietly unpacked that secret little van, and nobody saw her. Busy-Body had a dreadful night. It was windy and cold. He wasn't used to riding broomsticks. It was most uncomfortable, and very jerky, so he had to cling on tightly. He felt sure the stick was jerking on purpose.

When the sun came up, the broomstick landed, leaving Busy-Body stiff, cold and very angry. How dare Madam Soapsuds treat him like that! He'd find out all her secrets, no matter what!

Madam Soapsuds told everyone what had happened and they laughed. "How do you like riding at night?" they teased.

Busy-Body scowled. He hoped no one would like Madam Soapsuds. But they did like her, and very much too. She ran a fine laundry. They could take a bag of washing to her in the morning and have it back, washed, mangled, dried and ironed at tea-time. It was really wonderful.

She wouldn't let anyone watch her at work. "No," she said, "I like to work alone, thank you."

"She's got some special magic secret at work," said Busy-Body to everyone. "She couldn't possibly do all that washing herself. Why, she had seven bags of dirty linen to wash today, and a pile of blankets from Dame Twig. And hey presto! By tea-time they were all clean, dry and ironed!"

Busy-Body puzzled day and night over her secret. It might be magic machinery, or hundreds of tiny imp servants that had been in that van.

Madam Soapsuds had a big room in her house that nobody went into, called her Washing Room. Strange noises came from it, clankings, splashings and bumpings. "Can't I just peek inside and see?" asked her friend, Dame Twig. But Madam Soapsuds shook her head.

"No. It would be dangerous. Not even I go into that room. I just shake the dirty linen in there, shut the door and leave it. At tea-time I open the door, and there it is, clean, dry and ironed, piled neatly for me to take."

"Extraordinary," said Dame Twig. "Well, Madam Soapsuds, watch out for Busy-Body. He'll poke his nose into that room if he possibly can."

"He'll be sorry if he does," said Madam Soapsuds.

Busy-Body certainly meant to find
out the secret of that Washing Room.
He watched Madam Soapsuds from
the window of his cottage opposite,
every day. He knew that she did not

often go out during the week, but on Saturdays she went to visit her sister in the next village for the whole day.

"That's the day for me to go to her house," thought the elf. "She's away all day! I can get in through her window, because she always leaves it a little bit open. Oh ho, Madam Soapsuds, I'll soon know your secret and tell everyone! I'm sure it's one you're ashamed of, or you wouldn't hide it so carefully !"

That Saturday, Madam Soapsuds put on her best bonnet and shawl as usual, took a basket of goodies, and caught the bus to the next village. Busy-Body waited until the bus had left. He crept out of his cottage, and went round to the back of Madam Soapsuds' house. No one was about.

The sitting-room window was open as usual. He slid it up, and jumped inside. From the Washing Room he could hear curious sounds.

Slishy-sloshy, splish-splash-splosh. Creak-clank, creak! Flap-flap-flap! Drippitty, drip! Bump-bump-bump! He stood and listened to the noises, filled with curiosity. He must peep inside and see what was happening.

The door was shut tight. He turned the handle and the door opened. A puff of steam came out in his face. Busy-Body carefully put his head round the door, but he couldn't see a thing because it was so steamy.

He listened to the odd noises. Whatever could be making them?

He went cautiously inside. The door slammed shut behind him. Busy-Body turned in fright and tried to open it. But he couldn't! Ooooh!

The steam cleared a little, and he saw that the room was full of tubs of water, swirling steam, mangles that swung their rollers round fast and creaked and clanked, and hot irons that bumped their way over tables on which clothes were spreading themselves ready to be pressed.

No one was there. Everything was working at top speed by itself. The soap in the tubs made a tremendous lather, the scrubbing-brushes worked hard, the mangles pressed the water from clothes, the whirling fan that dried them rushed busily round and round up in the ceiling.

Busy-Body felt scared. He had never seen so much magic at work.

He felt himself pushed towards one of the tubs. In he went, splash, into the hot water. A large piece of soap ran over him and a big frothy lather appeared. He spluttered as soap went in his eyes and nose.

"Stop! Stop!" begged Busy-Body. But the magic couldn't stop. It was set to go, and go on it had to. Besides, it didn't often have a real person to wash, mangle and iron!

Poor Busy-Body was soaked in tub after tub, soaped and re-soaped, lathered, and scrubbed till he felt as if he was nothing but a bit of rag.

He was whizzed over to one of the mangles whose rollers were turning busily, squeezing the water out of the flattened clothes. Look out, Busy-Body!

He just managed to fling himself down below the mangle before he was put in between the rollers.

He crawled into a corner, and wept. Why had he bothered about Madam Soapsuds' horrid secret?

A tub rolled near him, splashing him with cold water. Then he was flung up to the ceiling, where he was hung on a wire to dry in the wind made by the magic fan, and then thrown back down to the floor.

Look out, Busy-Body! You are near the magic irons! Wheeeee! He was up on the ironing table, and a hot iron ran over his leg! Busy-Body squealed, and leapt off the table. Into a tub of hot water he went this time, and a big scrubbing-brush began to scrub him in delight. Then he was flung into a tub of cold water and rinsed well.

"I've never been so wet in my life! I've never had so much soap in my mouth and nose and eyes! Oh, how can I get away?"

It was lucky for Busy-Body that Madam Soapsuds came home early that day, or he would certainly have been mangled and ironed sooner or later. But suddenly the door opened, and a voice said:

"I have come for you, clothes!"

At once the clean, dry, mangled,

ironed clothes made neat piles by the door – and on top poor Busy-Body was flung, wet and dripping!

"Good gracious! What's this?" said Madam Soapsuds, in surprise. "You, Busy-Body! Serves you right for peeping and prying. You're not dry, mangled or ironed. Go back and be done properly."

"No, no!" squealed Busy-Body, afraid. "Let me go. Let me go!" Madam Soapsuds got hold of him.

He was dripping from head to foot. "Maybe I'll peg you up on my line in the garden instead," she said. And to Busy-Body's shame and

horror, she pegged him firmly up on her clothes line by the seat of his trousers – and there he swung in the wind, unable to get away.

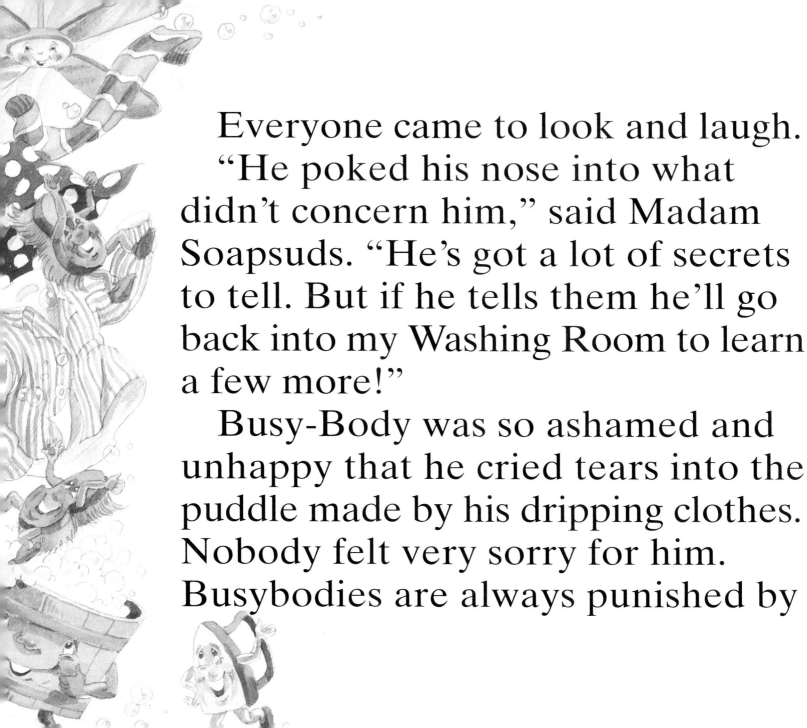

Everyone came to look and laugh.
"He poked his nose into what didn't concern him," said Madam Soapsuds. "He's got a lot of secrets to tell. But if he tells them he'll go back into my Washing Room to learn a few more!"

Busy-Body was so ashamed and unhappy that he cried tears into the puddle made by his dripping clothes. Nobody felt very sorry for him. Busybodies are always punished by themselves in the end!

"Now you can go," said Madam Soapsuds, at last, unpegging him. "And what are you going to do, Busy-Body? Are you going to run round telling my secrets?"

No. Busy-Body wasn't going to do anything of the sort. He didn't even want to think of that awful Washing Room. So he tried not to.

But he can't help dreaming about it, and when the neighbours hear him yelling at night, they laugh and say: "He thinks he's in that Washing Room again. Poor Busy-Body!"

Enid Blyton's

Peronel's Magic Polish

ILLUSTRATED BY SARA SILCOCK

Once upon a time there was a little fairy called Peronel. He lived in the King of Fairyland's palace, and his work was to clean all the brass that the Head Footman brought into the kitchen.

He was very good at this. He would sit all morning, and rub and polish away till the brass fire-irons and trays shone beautifully.

"That's very nice, Peronel," the cook would say to him every morning.

This made him very happy, and he beamed with pride. He thought that no one had ever polished brass as beautifully as he did.

One day, as Peronel sat polishing a brass coal bucket, he had a great idea.

"I know what I'll do!" he said. "I'll invent a new polish that will make everything twice as dazzling as before! I think I know just where to find the right ingredients. How delighted everyone will be!"

So that night he slipped out into the woods and gathered roots and leaves, and a magic flower that only blossomed at midnight, and two cobwebs just newly made. Then he went back to bed.

Next day he boiled everything together, strained it through the cook's sieve, and left it to cool. Then he went to the Wizened Witch, and asked her to sell him a little pot with a brightness spell inside. She told him:

"Empty this into your mixture at sunset, stir it well and sing these words:
'Now the magic has begun,
Polish brighter than the sun!'
Then everything you polish will be brighter than it ever was before!"

"Oh, thank you!" cried Peronel, and ran happily off clutching the little pot, after paying the Wizened Witch a bright new penny he had polished the day before.

When the sun sank slowly down in the sky, Peronel fetched his jar of polish. He emptied the Witch's Spell of Brightness into it, stirred it, and sang:

"Now the magic has begun,
Polish brighter than the sun!"

Next morning Peronel proudly put the polish he had made on the kitchen table, and started work. He had six brass candlesticks to clean and a table lamp. He worked very hard indeed for a whole hour until the cook came into the kitchen. She stopped and threw up her hands in great surprise.

"My goodness, Peronel!" she cried in astonishment. "What *have* you been doing to those candlesticks!

I can hardly look at them, they're so bright!"

"I'm using a magic polish, you see," said Peronel proudly. "Isn't it lovely! I made it all myself!"

The cook called the footmen and the ladies' maids and the butler, to see what a wonderful job Peronel had done.

"Look how bright Peronel has made the candlesticks!" she said. "Isn't he clever? He's made up a magic polish of his own!"

Everybody thought Peronel was certainly very clever indeed, and the little fairy was delighted. But he longed to do something that would make the King and Queen notice him too.

You'd never guess what he did! He fetched the King's golden crown in the middle of the night, and gave it a tremendous polishing with his magic polish! Then he quietly put it back again.

In the morning the King couldn't make out what had happened to his gleaming crown.

"It's so bright I can't bear to look at it," he said to the Queen. "It shines like the sun!"

"Put it on, then your eyes won't be dazzled," said the Queen, and the King took her advice.

But Peronel's polishing had not only made the crown bright, it had made it terribly slippery too, and it

wouldn't stay straight. It kept slipping, first over one ear, then over the other, and everybody in court began to giggle.

The King became quite cross.

"Well, I don't know who's been polishing my crown," he said, "but, anyway, I wish they wouldn't! It's a silly idea!"

Peronel was just nearby, and heard what the King said. Instead of being a sensible little fairy, and deciding not to try to make people praise him any more, he became quite angry.

"All right," he thought. "I'll polish something else tonight! Nobody will know who's done it, and I'll have a bit of fun!"

So the naughty little fairy took his polish and his cloth into the

King's breakfast room that night, and began polishing the gold chairs with all his might.

You can imagine what happened next morning! The King and Queen, the Princess and the Prince, all sat down to breakfast, but they couldn't sit still! They slid and slipped and slithered about on their chairs till the footmen standing behind nearly burst themselves with trying not to laugh!

When the King disappeared under the table, everybody thought it was very funny, even the Queen.

"Dear, dear, dear!" she laughed. "I never saw you disappear so quickly before! I really think we'd better sit on some other chairs until the polish has worn off! Goodness knows who has made them so shining and slippery!"

"I'll soon find out!" said the King crossly, looking very red in the face as he sat down on another chair.

"No, no, dear," said the Queen. "It was only an accident! Somebody's been doing his work too well!"

When Peronel heard what had happened, he was very pleased, and chuckled loudly. He wished he had seen it all.

"I'd like to polish something and see what happens *myself*," he thought. "Now, what can I polish? I know! There's a dance tomorrow night in the ballroom. I'll ask if I can help to polish the floor, and then I'll hide behind a curtain and see all the people slipping about!"

The naughty little fairy found it was quite easy to get permission to help. The other servants were only too glad to have him, for they all knew how quick and clever he was.

Whilst they were at dinner, he mixed a little of his magic polish into all their pots, and then ran in to his own dinner.

All afternoon Peronel and the other servants polished the floor in preparation for the dance, until it shone like sunlight.

"Dear me!" said the butler, peeping in. "You *have* all worked well!"

He came into the big room – and suddenly his legs slid from beneath him, and he sat down on the floor with a bump.

"Good gracious!" he cried. "Isn't the floor slippery!"

Peronel chuckled. Then he darted behind a curtain, waiting for the evening, when the guests would come in and dance.

At last they came, chattering and laughing. But, directly they began to dance on the slippery floor, their feet didn't seem to belong to them! They went slithering everywhere – then bumpity-bump, the guests began tumbling down, as if they were dancing on ice!

Just then the King came into the ballroom, and stared in the greatest astonishment to see half the dancers on the floor! "What is the matter?" he cried, striding forward.

He soon knew – for his feet flew from under him, and bump! He sat down suddenly.

"Who has polished the floor like this?" he thundered. "It's as slippery as ice. Fetch the servants. I shall punish them!"

Peronel trembled behind the curtain, and wondered what he should do. He wasn't a coward, and he knew he couldn't let the servants be punished for something that was his fault.

So, to the King's surprise, Peronel rushed out from behind the curtain, and ran up to where His Majesty still sat on the floor. But he forgot that it was slippery, and he suddenly slipped, turned head-over-heels, and landed right in the King's lap!

"Bless my buttons!" roared the King in fright. "Whatever's happened now!"

Very frightened indeed, Peronel got up off the King's lap and stood trembling as he confessed what he had done.

"It wasn't the other servants' fault; it was mine," he said. "And it was I who polished your crown the other day, but I only meant to be useful, truly I did!"

"You're a great deal too useful," said the King crossly, getting up very carefully. "You can choose your own punishment, Peronel. You can either stay in the Palace and never polish anything again, or leave the Palace and take your wonderful polish with you."

Sadly Peronel wondered what to do.

"I don't want to do anything else but polish," he said at last. "So I'm afraid I'll have to leave the Palace and take my magic polish with me."

And he did, and what do you suppose he does with it now?

He goes to the fields and meadows and polishes every single golden yellow buttercup that he finds. Look inside one, and you'll see how beautifully he does it!

He misses his friends at the Palace, but now he has made new friends with all the little creatures of the countryside, and he spends his days happily polishing to his heart's content!

Enid Blyton's
Redcap and the Broomstick Witch

ILLUSTRATED BY K. RAYMOND AND A. GREY

There was once a little gnome called Redcap, who lived right in the middle of Cuckoo Wood. His cottage was the cosiest little place, surrounded by trees and wild flowers. Redcap thought he was the luckiest little gnome in the world.

Early one morning he rang the little bell up on his roof to wake his friends for breakfast. Out of their holes peeped the bunnies. Squirrels scampered down from the trees.

The blackbirds and starlings came, and the robins and sparrows flew round, whistling and chirping.

Redcap gave them crumbs to eat and water to drink. He picked two of his finest lettuces for the bunnies, and gave the squirrels some nuts.

Then they sat in a ring and told each other the dreams they had had in the night.

When it came to Redcap's turn, he looked rather upset.

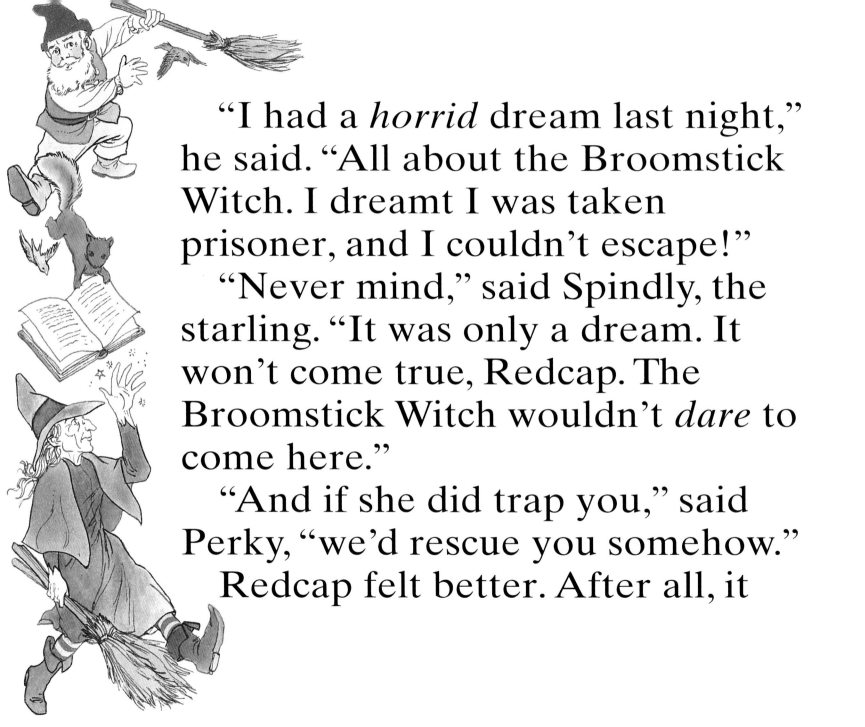

"I had a *horrid* dream last night," he said. "All about the Broomstick Witch. I dreamt I was taken prisoner, and I couldn't escape!"

"Never mind," said Spindly, the starling. "It was only a dream. It won't come true, Redcap. The Broomstick Witch wouldn't *dare* to come here."

"And if she did trap you," said Perky, "we'd rescue you somehow."

Redcap felt better. After all, it

was only a dream. He decided not to worry about it any more.

He ate breakfast with his friends, and soon forgot about the dream.

Later, Redcap was cooking dinner, when he heard someone walking through the wood calling out:

"Brooms for sale! Brooms for sale! Nice new brooms for sale!"

He peeped out of his window and saw an old woman with a shawl, walking up the path to his cottage.

Redcap remembered his dream. Perhaps this was the witch. Oh dear, oh dear!

"Never mind!" he thought. "She can't harm me here. Anyway, she doesn't look like a witch."

The old woman stopped at his window. "Would you like a nice new broom?" she asked.

"No, thank you," answered Redcap, though it wasn't *quite* the truth, for he did need a new broom.

He didn't want to buy one from an old woman who might be a witch though. You never knew what spell she might leave behind.

The old woman sighed, and put the brooms over her shoulder again. Then she sniffed at the smell of Redcap's soup.

"Oh!" she said. "How delicious that smells! I am so hungry, and I've sold no brooms today."

"Well," thought Redcap, "it can't do any harm to give her some soup." He called her inside.

When she had eaten her meal, the old woman thanked Redcap,

got up, and went on her way with her load of broomsticks. Later, when Redcap went outside he stared in astonishment – for leaning against his gate was a brand new broom!

Redcap took it and swept his garden path. It was a fine broom, and swept as clean as could be.

"Perky! Spindly! Bobtail!" called Redcap joyfully. "Come and see what I've got!"

All his friends gathered round.

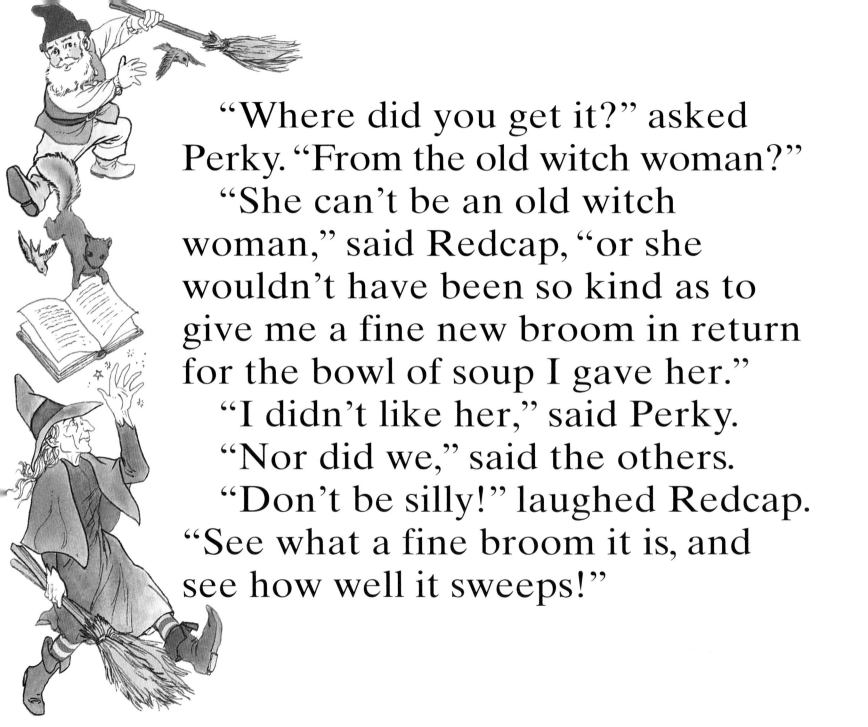

"Where did you get it?" asked Perky. "From the old witch woman?"

"She can't be an old witch woman," said Redcap, "or she wouldn't have been so kind as to give me a fine new broom in return for the bowl of soup I gave her."

"I didn't like her," said Perky.

"Nor did we," said the others.

"Don't be silly!" laughed Redcap. "See what a fine broom it is, and see how well it sweeps!"

He began to sweep his path again – but oh dear! What do you think happened?

The broom suddenly rose in the air and *flew away with Redcap*!

"Oh!" he cried. "It's magic! It's taking me to the Broomstick Witch!"

"Perky! Climb to the tree-tops and follow him!" called Bobtail to the little squirrel. Perky leapt into the nearest tree, and soon was lost from sight.

"I *knew* she was a horrid old woman!" sighed Bobtail. "Poor Redcap! Whatever can we do?"

"We must wait until Perky comes back," said Spindly. So they waited, feeling very worried.

After a whole hour had gone by, Perky returned, out of breath.

"I followed the broom!" he panted, "and I've never travelled so fast in my life! It's gone to Red Chimney Cottage on Witchy Hill. It flew down to the garden, and as soon as it touched the ground, that old witch-woman came out and tied poor Redcap up. Then she took him indoors and I came back here!"

"Dear, dear!" said Bobtail. "We must rescue him. We promised we would if anything happened to him."

"Let's go and hide near Red Chimney Cottage," said Spindly. "We might find some way to save him tonight, when the witch is out."

So when the sun had set the little band of birds and bunnies set out, guided by Perky, who knew the way.

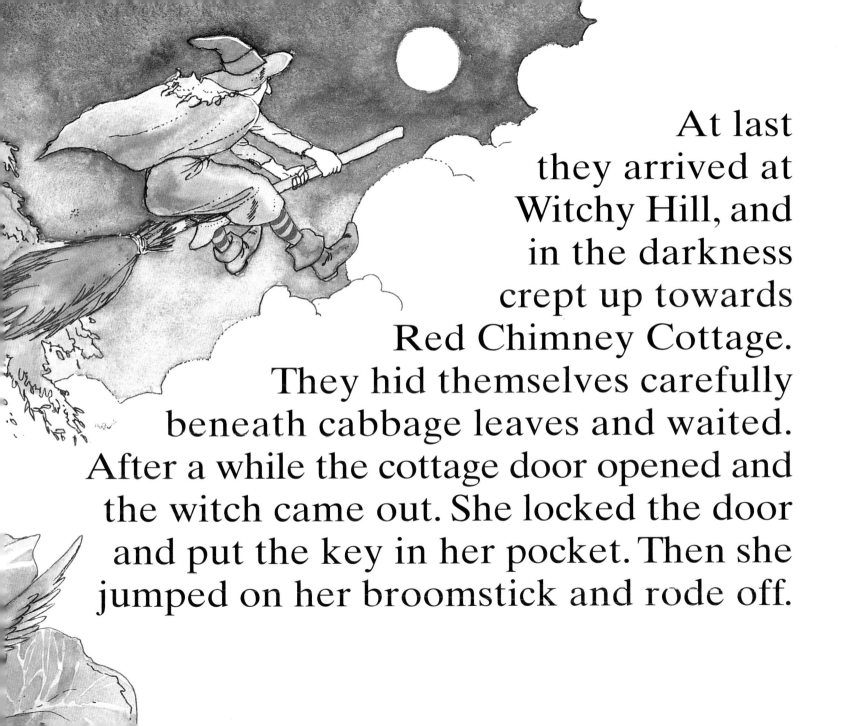

At last they arrived at Witchy Hill, and in the darkness crept up towards Red Chimney Cottage. They hid themselves carefully beneath cabbage leaves and waited. After a while the cottage door opened and the witch came out. She locked the door and put the key in her pocket. Then she jumped on her broomstick and rode off.

Quickly Redcap's friends ran out
from their hiding places and went
up to the cottage door.

"Redcap! Redcap!" called Perky.
"Are you in there?"

"Yes!" answered Redcap. "Oh! I *am* so glad to hear you. The witch has tied me up to keep me prisoner. She wants me to help her with her bad spells, and I won't."

"Don't worry," said Bobtail. "We'll save you. We just need to find a way to get in."

They tried the door, but it was locked tight.

"Try the window!" said Redcap.

Perky jumped up on the window-sill, but there were strong bars, and no one could get in or out *that* way.

Everyone was very worried.

"We *must* do something soon, or the witch will be back!" said Perky.

"Let's all think hard!"

"I know!" cried Bobtail. "What about going down the chimney? Look, there's a tree that hangs over the roof, Perky. Couldn't you climb up, and pop down the chimney? There's no fire tonight, for the chimney isn't smoking."

"Good idea!" cried Perky, scurrying up the tree. "I'll nibble his ropes in two and Redcap will soon be free!"

In no time the little squirrel was down the chimney. He ran to where Redcap lay in a corner, tied tightly up with ropes. How glad he was to see Perky!

"Now for a good nibble!" said the squirrel, and began gnawing at the ropes as hard as he could.

One by one they fell apart, and soon Redcap was free!

"Oh! thank you, Perky," he said. "Now, how can I get out?"

He looked around in a dreadful panic, then spotted the witch's spell-book, and magic wand on the shelf. He took the big book down, put it on the table and opened it. He found the spell he needed, and turning to face the door, said:

"Abracadabra, quick as can be,
Please unlock this door for me!"
At once, the door sprang open! All his friends outside crowded round him in delight.

"Come home quickly," they said, "before the witch comes back."

"Hold on," said Redcap. "I have an idea."

He went back inside and brought out all the brooms he could find.

"Listen!" he said. "A witch is no good without her brooms. Take one each and sit on it. There are enough brooms for everyone but me."

"But we can't leave you behind, Redcap!" cried everyone.

"You won't have to!" said the gnome, chuckling. "I shall hide in the garden till the witch comes back. When she gets off *her* broom and goes inside, I shall take it quickly, say the magic rhyme, and off we'll all

go as quick
as lightning,
leaving her behind!"
"What a splendid
idea!" cried Bobtail.
"Then she'll be harmless,
and we'll all get a good
ride home. What fun!"
"Sh! Sh!" suddenly said Perky.
"She's coming! Hide quickly!"
They took the broomsticks
to the long grass. Redcap hid

among some hollyhocks near the door, and waited.

Down flew the witch on her broomstick, and landed by the door.

She jumped off and leaned it up against the wall just near Redcap. Then she felt in her pocket to find the key. At the same moment Redcap gave a tremendous yell, snatched the broom and jumped on it. His friends did the same, and the witch fell over backwards in fright.

"Broomstick, fly
Away to the sky;
High and then low,
Away we go!"

As Redcap sang these magic words the broomsticks rose in the air and flew to Cuckoo Wood. The old witch called them, but they wouldn't go back to *her* any more!

When the friends arrived home after a fine ride, they chuckled in delight to know their little friend was safe once more. Redcap thanked them again and again.

"Now put your broomsticks in a heap," he said, "and we'll burn them. Then the old witch can do no more harm!"

The broomsticks were so full of magic that as they burnt the flames were green and the smoke was red.

Then the friends went to bed, and settled down happily to sleep, knowing they would have breakfast together in the morning, and they didn't need to worry about the Broomstick Witch any more!

Enid Blyton's
A Tale of Shuffle, Trot and Merry

ILLUSTRATED BY KATE DAVIES

"Now come along!" shouted Mr Smarty. "Where are you, Shuffle, Trot and Merry? I've some shopping here ready for you to take to my house!" They were playing marbles in a corner of the market.

Shuffle groaned. "Blow! Now we've got to put his sacks of shopping on our backs and walk for miles to his house. I'm tired of it! Why doesn't he buy a horse and cart for us to drive?"

"Because it's too expensive," said Trot. "Come along – he'll be cross if we don't hurry."

They went over to Mr Smarty, who was standing by three big sacks.

"Oh – so there you are, you lazy lot!" he said. "I've bought all these things at the market, and I want them taken to my house as fast as possible."

"It's too hot to walk fast with big sacks like those!" said Shuffle.

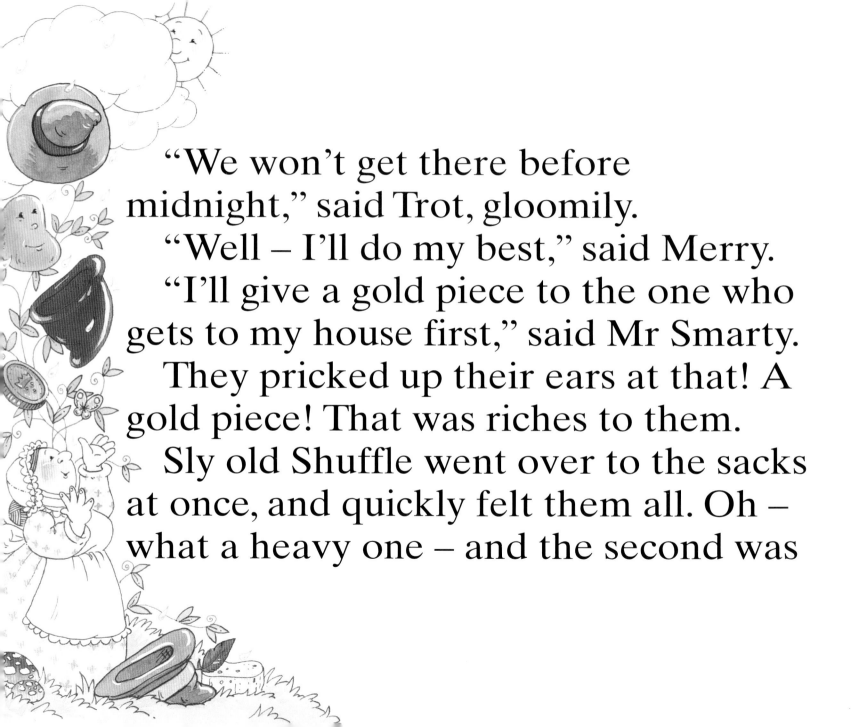

"We won't get there before midnight," said Trot, gloomily.

"Well – I'll do my best," said Merry.

"I'll give a gold piece to the one who gets to my house first," said Mr Smarty.

They pricked up their ears at that! A gold piece! That was riches to them.

Sly old Shuffle went over to the sacks at once, and quickly felt them all. Oh – what a heavy one – and the second was heavy too – but the third one felt as light as a feather! That was the one for him!

"I shall hardly know I've a sack on my back!" he thought. "I'll easily be the first one there and I'll get the gold piece!"

He shuffled off with the very light sack on his back.

Trot went over to the two sacks left, wondering what was in them.

He stuck a finger into one – it was full of something round and hard – potatoes, perhaps? He stuck a finger into the other and felt

something loose and soft – what
was it – flour – salt – sugar? He
pulled out his finger and sucked it.
It tasted sweet and delicious.

"Ah – sugar!" he said. "Lovely! I can cut a tiny hole in the sack and dip my finger into the sugar all the time I'm walking along. What a treat!"

So Trot took the second sack and set off to catch up with Shuffle. Merry whistled a happy tune and went to

the sack that was left. He made a face as he lifted it on to his back. "It's heavy – full of potatoes, I think – probably covered in mud too, which makes them twice as heavy. Well – here goes – I must catch up Shuffle and Trot before they get too far, or I won't win that gold piece!"

But it was difficult to catch up with Shuffle, even though he was not the fastest walker as a rule – because his sack was so very, very light. Shuffle had no idea what was inside, and he didn't care. He was delighted to have picked such a light load!

"That gold piece is as good as in my pocket!" he thought. "And I'm going to keep it all for myself!"

Trot was having quite a good time with his sack, as he trotted along eating the sugar. What a joke, he thought – he was lightening his load and having a feast at the same time!

Merry walked fast, but his load was really heavy – and then he had the bad luck to stub his toe on a big stone, and that made him limp!

"Just my luck!" he groaned. "I'll never catch up with the others now – I can't walk fast with a sore toe!"

So Merry fell behind, but all the same he whistled a merry tune and smiled at anyone he passed. But soon clouds began to cover the sun,

and a wind blew up and made the trees sway to and fro. Then Merry felt a drop of rain on his face and he sighed.

"Now it's going to pour with rain and I shall get soaked. I'd better give up all hope of getting that gold piece!"

The rain began to pelt down, stinging the faces of the three little fellows. Shuffle was a great way ahead of the others, and he grinned as he looked round and saw how far behind they were.

But, as the rain poured down, odd things began to happen! First of all, Shuffle's sack grew heavier!

"Is my sack getting heavy, or am I just imagining it?" he thought.

He walked a little further and then felt that he must have a rest. "My sack feels twice as heavy! Whatever can be inside?" He set it down and untied the rope.

He put in his hand and felt something soft, squashy and wet! The rain had gone right into the sack. Can you guess what it was inside?

It was a sponge! "No wonder the sack felt so light when the sponges were dry!" said Shuffle, in dismay. "Now they're soaked with rain and as heavy as can be! What can I do?"

Trot came along grinning. "Hello Shuffle – so your load was sponges, was it? It serves you right for

picking the lightest load as usual.
Now you've got the heaviest!"

"What's in your sack?"
called Shuffle, annoyed,
but Trot didn't stop.
No, he saw a chance
of winning that
gold piece now.
He was going
quite fast.
Also his sack
felt lighter!

In fact, it soon felt so light that Trot stopped in surprise. "What's happening?" he thought. "My sack feels remarkably light!"

He set it down to see – and, to his horror, he found that the sugar was all melting in the rain and dripping fast out of the bottom of the sack!

"I ought to get under cover, or it will all be melted away," thought Trot, in dismay. "Why didn't I remember that sugar melts? Well,

I've outpaced old Shuffle – but if I wait till the rain stops Merry will be sure to catch me up and pass me, and I shan't get that gold piece."

So on he went in the pouring rain, while the sugar in his sack melted faster than ever. But at least he was now in the lead!

As for Merry he still whistled in the pouring rain, for he was a light-hearted fellow. The rain ran into his sack, down among the potatoes and soon muddy water was dripping out at the bottom. Merry laughed.

"You're washing all the dirty potatoes for me!" he said to the rain clouds above. "Hello – there's Shuffle in front of me – he's very slow today!"

He soon passed Shuffle, who groaned loudly as Merry passed him. "My load is sponges!" he shouted. "And they're four times

as heavy as they were now that they're soaked with rain."

"Serves you right!" said Merry. "You picked the lightest sack so that you could win that gold piece!"

The three went on through the rain, and at last came one by one to Mr Smarty's big house. Trot arrived at the back door first and set down his sack on the ground.

"Hello!" said the cook. "Have you brought something for the master?

"I'll tell him you were the first to arrive."

The next was Merry with his sack of potatoes. The cook peered at them and smiled. "Well I never – the potatoes are all washed clean for me! That's a good mark for you, Merry."

Last of all came poor Shuffle, very weary with carrying such a wet and heavy load. He set his sack down and water from the sponges ran all over the floor.

"Now pick up that sack and stand it outside!" said the cook. "My floor's in enough mess already without you making it a running river. What in the world have you got in that sack?"

But Shuffle was too tired to answer. The cook gave them all some food

and drink and they sat back and
waited to be seen by Mr Smarty.
At last they were sent for, and
the cook took them in to his study.

"Here's the one who arrived first," she said, pushing Trot forward. His sack looked limp, wet and empty. Mr Smarty glared at it in rage.

"What's this? It should be full of sugar! Where's the sugar, Trot? Have you sold it to someone on the way?"

"No, sir. The rain melted it," said Trot. "I was here first, sir. Can I have my gold piece?"

"Bah! You don't deserve it." said Mr Smarty. "Why didn't you get under cover and save my expensive sugar?" Then he turned to Shuffle.

"Shuffle, you were third, so you're out of it. Take that disgustingly dripping sack out of the room. Merry, what about you?"

"Sir, he's brought potatoes – and they're all washed clean!" said the cook, eagerly, for she liked Merry. "He deserves the gold piece, even though he wasn't the first here!"

Merry laughed. "The rain did the cleaning!" he said.

"You weren't the first," said Mr Smarty, "but you certainly delivered my goods in a better condition

than when I bought them – so I shall award the gold piece for that." He tossed a shining coin to the delighted Merry, who went happily off to the kitchen. What sulks and grumbles met him from Shuffle and Trot! He clapped them on the shoulder.

"Cheer up – we'll go and spend my gold piece together. What's good luck for but to be shared!"

They all went out arm in arm and the cook stared after them, smiling.

"You deserve good luck, Merry!" she called. "And you'll always get it – a merry face and a generous heart are the luckiest things in the world!"
I think she could be right.

Enid Blyton's

The Magic Bicycle

ILLUSTRATED BY ANGELA KINCAID

Peter had a lovely new bicycle for his birthday. It was painted bright red with a yellow seat, and on the handlebars was a bright silver bell.

It was a fine bell, and had a very loud ring. You should have seen everybody jump when Peter cycled up and rang it just behind them.

Peter went out on his bicycle
every day after school, just before
tea. It was great fun cycling up and
down the lane, ring-ringing all
the way.

But one afternoon a strange thing happened to Peter. He was cycling along whistling happily to himself, watching rabbits scamper along the grassy verge.

When he came to the little hill that ran down to the sweet-shop at the bottom, he took both his feet off the pedals and had a lovely ride – but, do you know, when he reached the bottom of the hill the bicycle wouldn't stop.

No, it went on, all by itself without Peter doing anything to help it. He was so surprised.

"What a funny thing!" he thought. "What's happened to my bicycle, why is it going by itself? Ooh! It's going faster! My goodness, I hope we don't run into anyone."

On and on went the little red bicycle, with Peter holding on tightly. It went faster and faster, and Peter had to hold on tightly to his cap, in case it blew away.

The bicycle raced through the village and made everyone jump quickly out of the way. It nearly knocked over Mister Plod, the policeman. Poor Peter couldn't possibly say he was sorry because the bicycle didn't stop.

On and on it went, up hills and down hills, along the country lanes, past fields and farmyards. At last the little red bicycle ran into a village Peter had never seen before. It was a strange place. The houses all looked like dolls' houses, and there was a farm exactly like Peter's toy farm in the nursery at home with funny wooden-looking trees standing in rows, and wooden-looking cows grazing in the fields.

And what do think were in the
street? – why, toys, all standing
about and talking to one another,
or shopping busily.

"This must be Toy Town," said Peter to himself, in great surprise. "Perhaps my bicycle came from here and felt homesick suddenly, and raced back home."

In the middle of the street was a wooden policeman, holding up his hand to stop the traffic. The bicycle tried to get past – but the policeman grabbed the handlebars and stopped it. Off fell Peter, landing with a bump.

"Why didn't you stop?" cried the policeman, crossly. "Didn't you see my hand put out?"

"Yes, but my bicycle wouldn't stop," said Peter. "It won't do what I tell it to!"

"I don't believe a word of it," said the policeman, getting out his notebook. "Show me your bicycle licence, please."

"But I haven't got one," said Peter, in surprise. "You don't need to have a bicycle licence where I come from – you only have licences for motor cars and television sets."

"In Toy Town you have to have a licence for bicycles too," said the policeman, sharply.

"You must come to the police-station with me, and pay a fine." "But I haven't any money," said Peter, quite frightened.

"Never mind," said the policeman. "You can pay your fine in chocolate money instead."

"I don't have any chocolate money either," wailed Peter. But it made no difference. The policeman took him by the arm, and marched him down the street. Suddenly there came a great noise of shouting not far off, and a big brown teddy bear rushed by, carrying a little bottle of brightly coloured sweets.

"Stop thief, stop thief!" cried a little wooden shopkeeper dressed in a stripy apron. And all the toys standing around in the street began to chase the teddy bear, but he jumped into a toy motor car and whizzed off at top speed.

Two more toy policemen rushed up. "Who has another motor car that we can use to chase him?" they cried. But nobody had. Then Peter had a fine idea.

"I'll go after him on my bicycle!" he said. "Jump up behind me, policemen, and I'll scoot after that naughty teddy."

In a trice he was back on his bicycle, and behind him crowded the three wooden policemen, and another teddy bear who wanted to join in the fun.

Peter pedalled as fast as he could, and soon he could see the teddy bear up ahead of him in the toy motor car.

The teddy looked behind him
and saw that he was being chased.
He went faster still, but Peter
pedalled as hard as he could and
soon he had nearly caught up.

Suddenly the clockwork motor car the teddy was driving began to run down. It went slower and slower, until finally it stopped. The teddy got out to wind it up again – but before he had given it more than one wind, Peter had pedalled alongside.

The policemen jumped off and grabbed the naughty teddy. They made him give up the bottle of sweets and said he must clean the whole sweet shop from top to bottom to show that he was sorry.

"Well," said the wooden policeman who had stopped Peter when he first arrived in the little village, "that was a very good idea of yours, to let us chase that teddy on your bicycle."

"That's quite all right," said Peter. "I was glad to help."

"Thanks very much anyway," said the policeman. "I won't say any more about your not having a bicycle licence. You can go home now – but please be sure to have a licence if you come to Toy Town again."

"Thank you," said Peter, sitting down on the grassy roadside. He was very hot and tired after his long cycle ride.

"It's been a great adventure. But I do wish I didn't have to cycle all the way home again. This bicycle of mine won't seem to go by itself any more, and I shall have to pedal it up all of those hills."

"Dear me, I didn't think about your being tired," said the policeman, very much upset. "Look here – get into this car with me – the one the teddy used. You can put your bicycle in the back. Can you drive a car?"

"No," said Peter, "not even a toy one, I'm afraid."

"What a nuisance," said the policeman. "I can't drive either." Then the clever policeman had a wonderful idea.

"Hey, Teddy Bear!" he cried to the miserable bear who was still being marched off down the road. "You can drive this car, can't you? You can do something else useful to make up for all the trouble you've caused."

"Oh! Yes," said the bear, pleased to show how clever he was. "Jump in everyone, and I'll drive Peter all the way home, if he will tell me where he lives."

Off they all went, right through Toy Town and back to the village where Peter lived. How his friends stared when they saw him drive up with three wooden policemen and two teddy bears – but before they could ask them any questions the

toys had driven off again, and Peter was left standing by his gate with his little red bicycle.

"What an adventure," he said. And it certainly was, wasn't it?

Enid Blyton's
The Yellow Trumpets

ILLUSTRATED BY K. RAYMOND AND A. GREY

Once upon a time there were two little elves who lived in Fairyland and made trumpets. They made all sorts of lovely trumpets – big ones, little ones, long ones, short ones, white ones, red ones and blue ones.

They sold them as fast as they made them, because the baby fairies loved blowing them, and were always coming to buy them.

"One penny, please," said Flip, giving a brownie a red one.

All day long they sold them in their little shop, and when night came they shut the shop and sat down to make more.

Soon every fairy baby, little elf, and tiny pixie had a trumpet, and you should have heard the noise in the streets and houses of Fairyland.

"Tan-tan-tara! Tan-tan-tara!"

It was the baby trumpeters blowing their trumpets.

The older fairies didn't mind at first. They liked the babies to amuse themselves and have fun. They put up with the noise and laughed.

But one day Pinkle discovered a way to make a trumpet which made such a loud noise that any passer-by nearly jumped out of his skin when he heard it!

It was a large, wide, yellow trumpet, beautifully made. Pinkle was very pleased with it.

"Flip!" he called. "Come here, and see my new trumpet!"

Flip hurried to see it. Pinkle showed the trumpet to him, then

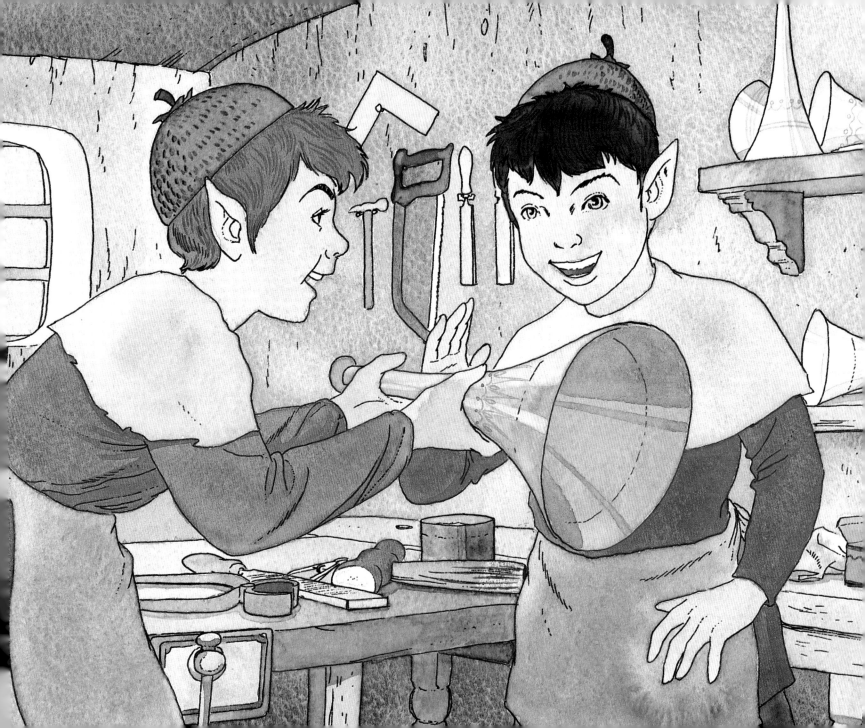

hid himself behind the window curtains.

When a gnome came hurrying by the window, carrying his morning's shopping, Pinkle blew his yellow trumpet loudly.

"Tan-tan-tan-TARA!" it went, right in the gnome's ear. He had never in his life heard such a tremendous noise.

He jumped into the air in fright, dropped his basket of shopping, and went scurrying down the street as fast as he could, feeling quite sure that some dreadful animal was roaring at him.

Pinkle and Flip laughed till they cried.

"Let's show the trumpet to the babies!" said Pinkle. "They're sure to want one each, and we will charge them sixpence!"

"Oh yes," said Flip in delight. "Then we will be so rich that we'll

never need to make any more
trumpets, and we'll go
away and have a lazy
time for the rest
of our lives!"

So the two naughty elves showed the baby fairies their new trumpet, and told them what fun they could have frightening everyone.

The little fairies thought it was a lovely idea, and sounded like great fun, and so did the baby pixies. They asked Pinkle and Flip to make them each one, and agreed that they would pay them sixpence.

So the two elves set to work, and by the next day they had made twelve, and sold them all for sixpence each.

Then what a noise there was in the streets of Fairyland! "Tan-tan-TARA! Tan-tan-TARA!"

The new trumpets nearly deafened everyone, and made people jump in fright.

"This won't do at all," said the King of the fairies. "We must stop this. We don't mind the little trumpets, but these big trumpets are too noisy. Pinkle and Flip must not make any more."

So a message was sent to tell the two elves they must not make any more of the big yellow trumpets.

They were terribly disappointed. What a shame not to make any more, just as they were getting so rich through selling them! Oh dear, oh dear!

Pinkle and Flip talked about the message very crossly, and then Flip suddenly whispered something in Pinkle's big left ear:

"Let's go on making them and selling them anyway. We'll tell the customers to come at night, and no one will know. Shall we, Pinkle?"

Pinkle nodded.

"Yes! We won't take any notice of their silly message. We'll make lots and lots more, and sell them every night when it's dark."

So when their little customers came to the shop, the naughty elves whispered to them to come and buy their yellow trumpets at midnight, if they really badly wanted them.

And night after night naughty little fairies and mischievous little pixies came creeping to Pinkle's back door, paid sixpence, and took away a trumpet.

Pinkle and Flip became
richer and richer, and Fairyland
became noisier and noisier.

At last the older fairies became really angry. They couldn't even sleep at night because of all the noise. But although they watched Pinkle and Flip's shop carefully every single day, they never *once* saw the elves sell one of those big yellow trumpets that made such a dreadful noise. They couldn't understand it. Where *did* the trumpets come from if Pinkle and Flip didn't make them?

"I know what we'll do," said one of the fairies. "We'll go to Flip and Pinkle's shop, and search it from top to bottom. Then we shall know if they have been making the trumpets. If they haven't, we must look somewhere else! We'll go as soon as the shop is open tomorrow!"

Now, that night when a little elf came to buy a trumpet, he told them what he had heard, and the two naughty elves were terribly frightened.

They knew that if they were found out, they might be sent right away from Fairyland, and they didn't want *that* to happen.

"What shall we do, what shall we do?" cried Pinkle. "We've nowhere to hide the trumpets!"

Flip thought for a minute.

"I know," he said, "We'll hide them in the fields. Quick, bring as many as you can!"

The two elves hurried out to the

fields, where a great many yellow flowers were growing.

"If we stick our trumpets into the middle of these yellow flowers, no one will guess where they are!" said Flip. "Come on!"

And quickly he began pushing a big yellow trumpet into each yellow-petalled flower. They matched beautifully!

When all the trumpets were hidden, the two elves went back to

their shop. It was just time to open it, so they unbolted the door.

In came the King of the fairies, and told Pinkle and Flip they were going to search the house from top to bottom.

"Certainly!" said Pinkle politely. "Please do! You won't find a single yellow trumpet here!"

And they didn't! Not one! But just as they were going away again, feeling very puzzled, a pixie came running in.

"Come and see the lovely yellow flowers in the field!" he cried. "They are wonderful! We've never seen anything like them before!"

Off went everyone to see them,

and Pinkle and Flip were taken along too.

But when the fairies looked at them carefully, they saw what made the flowers look strange and beautiful – they each had a yellow trumpet in the midst of their petals!

"So *that's* where you hid them, you rascals!" cried the fairies, and caught hold of Pinkle and Flip angrily. "Out of Fairyland you shall go!"

"No, no!" wept Pinkle and Flip

miserably. "Please let us stay. We'll never, *never*, NEVER make big yellow trumpets again!"

Suddenly a fairy had a great idea.

"I know!" he cried. "Let's allow Pinkle and Flip to go on making their trumpets for these flowers! See how much more beautiful they are with the long trumpets in the middle!"

"Yes, yes!" cried all the fairies and pixies.

So it was settled. And from that day to this, Pinkle and Flip had to work hard to make the big yellow trumpets for the loveliest yellow flowers of the spring.

You have seen them often, for daffodils grow in everybody's garden – and if you look carefully at them next springtime, you will see how beautifully Pinkle and Flip have made their yellow trumpets.